Roger
Lancelyn Green

Robin Hood and
His Merry Men

D1136822

PENGUIN BOOKS

PENGUIN BOOKS

Published by the Penguin Group
Penguin Books Ltd, 27 Wrights Lane, London W8 5TZ, England
Penguin Books USA Inc., 375 Hudson Street, New York, New York 10014, USA
Penguin Books Australia Ltd, Ringwood, Victoria, Australia
Penguin Books Canada Ltd, 10 Alcorn Avenue, Toronto, Ontario, Canada M4V 3B2
Penguin Books (NZ) Ltd, 182–190 Wairau Road, Auckland 10, New Zealand

Penguin Books Ltd, Registered Offices: Harmondsworth, Middlesex, England

First published in *The Adventures of Robin Hood* in Puffin Books 1956

This collection published in Penguin Books 1996
1 3 5 7 9 10 8 6 4 2

Set in 12.5/14.5pt Bembo Monotype
Typeset by Datix International Limited, Bungay, Suffolk
Printed in England by Clays Ltd, St Ives plc

Contents

1 How Little John Came to the Greenwood 1

2 How Sir Richard of Legh Paid the Abbot 13

3 Maid Marian of Sherwood Forest 26

4 The Coming of Friar Tuck 45

How Little John Came to the Greenwood

AFTER Robin Hood had rescued Will Scarlet from the Sheriff of Nottingham, he remained quietly in Sherwood Forest for some time, building huts in several of the most secret and hidden clearings, drilling his followers and teaching those who were new to it all the secrets of woodlore.

Many came to swell his band, outlaws, poor men who were suffering under cruel masters, and even a yeoman or two and several who had been forced into the service of the Sheriff or of various of the Norman knights and barons of the district.

The Great North Road passed through the Forest at that time, and surprise attacks supplied them with all they needed in the way of Lincoln green cloth and arrows – or the money with which to buy these.

When order and comfort had been brought to this new commonwealth of the greenwood, and precautions taken against surprise by the Sheriff or any of the neighbouring knights such as Sir Guy of Gisborne and their followers, Robin began to go further afield. He knew that it would be well to have several places of refuge should Prince John send a large force to drive him out of Sherwood, and in time he and his men were able to disappear from the Nottingham district, and were often to be found in Barnsdale, Yorkshire, or Plompton in Cumberland: on occasion they were known even to visit Pendle Forest in Lancashire and Delamere Forest in Cheshire.

Much of their time was taken up in archery at which all became very proficient, though none could ever shoot so far or so true as Robin himself; and in fencing with swords, or playing at quarterstaff. But there was time for hunting as well, since venison was the most usual food, varied with pork from the wild boars, hares, and various wild fowl.

Many a time Robin would grow weary of the general course of every day and wander off by himself, leaving Will Scarlet in command. Often he returned from these expeditions with news of a party of wealthy travellers to be waylaid and robbed, or of some new injustice or cruelty practised against a Saxon yeoman or Saxon serfs. Sometimes he returned with a new member for his band of outlaws – and the most noteworthy of these chance meetings won for him the truest and most faithful of all his friends.

It was late in their first summer in Sherwood, and on a sudden Robin grew restless.

'Stay you all here, my merry fellows,' he said early one morning. 'But come and come swiftly if you hear the blast on my horn that you all know as my special call. We have had no sport these fourteen days and more: no adventure has befallen us – so I will go forth and seek for one. But if I should find myself in difficulties, with no escape, then will I blow my horn.'

Then he bade farewell to Scarlet and the rest, 3

and set off blithely through the greenwood, his bow ready in his hand, his eyes and ears alert for anything of danger or of interest.

About noon he came along a forest path to a wide, swiftly flowing stream which was crossed by a narrow bridge made of a single tree-trunk flattened on the top. As he approached it, he saw a tall yeoman hastening towards him beyond the stream.

'We cannot both cross at once, the bridge is too narrow,' thought Robin, and he quickened his pace meaning to be first over.

But the tall yeoman quickened his pace also, with the result that they each set foot on the opposite ends of the bridge at the same moment.

'Out of my way, little man!' shouted the stranger, who was a good foot taller than Robin. 'That is, unless you want a ducking in the stream!'

'Not so fast, not so fast, tall fellow,' answered Robin. 'Go you back until I have passed – or may be I will do the ducking!'

'Why then,' cried the stranger, waving his staff, 'I'll break your head first, and tip you into the water afterwards!'

'We'll see about that,' said Robin, and taking an arrow well feathered from the wing of a goose, he fitted it to the string.

'Draw that bow string ever so little!' shouted the stranger, 'and I'll first tan your hide with this good staff of mine, and then soak you well in the stream!'

'You talk like a plain ass!' exclaimed Robin scornfully, 'for were I to bend my bow I could send an arrow quite through your proud heart before you could touch me with your staff.'

'If I talk like an ass,' answered the stranger, 'you talk like a coward. You stand there well armed with a good long bow, while I have only a staff and am well out of your reach.'

'I scorn the name of coward,' cried Robin, slipping the arrow back into his quiver and unstringing his bow. 'Therefore will I lay aside my weapons and try your manhood with a quarter- 5 staff such as your own — if you will but wait there until I cut one in the thicket.'

'Here I bide,' said the stranger cheerfully, 'one foot on the bridge — until you are ready for your cold bath in the stream!'

Robin Hood stepped aside to a thicket of trees and chose himself a stout six-foot staff of ground oak, straight and true and strong. Then he returned to the bridge, lopping and trimming his weapon as he came. He flung his bow and quiver on the bank, with his hood and his horn beside them, and set foot again on the bridge, crying merrily:

'Lo what a lusty staff I have, and a tough one at that — the very thing for knocking insolent rogues into the water! Let us fight here on the bridge, so that if one of us goes into the water, there will be no doubt who has won, and the victor may go on his way without a wetting.'

'With all my heart,' said the stranger. 'I scorn to give way . . . Have at your head!' So saying, he 6 grasped his staff one quarter of the way from the end, held his other hand ready to grasp it by the middle when using it as a shield, and advanced along the narrow bridge.

Robin came to meet him, flourishing his weapon round his head, and by a quick feint got the end in under his adversary's guard and made his ribs ring with the blow.

'This must be repaid!' cried the stranger. 'Be sure I'll give you as good as I get for so long as I am able to handle a staff – and I scorn to die in your debt when a good crack will pay what I owe!'

Then they went at it with mighty blows, rather as if threshing corn with flails. Presently the sharp rattle and clatter of wood upon wood was broken by a duller crack as the stranger struck Robin on the head, causing the blood to appear; and after that they lashed at each other all the more fiercely, Robin beating down the guard and getting in with blow after blow on shoulders and sides until the dust flew from the stranger's jerkin like smoke.

But on a sudden, with a great cry of rage, the stranger whirled up his staff and smote so mightily and with such fury that even Robin could not withstand it, but tumbled head over heels into the stream and disappeared from sight.

'Good fellow, good fellow, where are you now?' shouted the stranger, kneeling on the bridge and gazing anxiously down into the water.

'Here I am!' shouted Robin gaily as he pulled himself out by an overhanging hawthorn, 'just floating down the stream – and washing my bruised head as I go! I must acknowledge myself beaten: you're a fine fellow, and a good hitter – and as the day is yours, let there be no more battle between us.'

With that Robin picked up his horn and sounded a shrill blast on it. Then turning to the stranger he said:

'Whither were you hastening in the greenwood? I trust that you can spare time from your business to dine with me? Indeed I insist upon it

– and must use force, if persuasion will not bring you!'

'To tell you truth,' answered the stranger, 'I was in search of a man they call Robin Hood –'

Before Robin could answer there was a crashing in the thicket and out bounded Will Scarlet, followed by many another of his men, making a bold show in their well-fitting doublets and hose of Lincoln green.

'Good master!' cried Scarlet, 'what has befallen you that you blew the call for us? You are bleeding – and wet to the skin!'

'Nothing has befallen me,' answered Robin, 'save that this fine fellow here has just tumbled me into the stream with that long staff of his!'

'By the Rood,' exclaimed Scarlet, 'he cannot go scot free after so insulting bold Robin Hood. Come on, my merry men, let us give him a turn of the cold water.'

'No, no!' laughed Robin. 'He's a stout fellow, and tumbled me over in fair fight – so let him be. Come now, my friend,' he added, turning to the 9 stranger, 'these bowmen will give you no cause for fear – they are all my friends. And they shall be your friends too, if you'll set your hand in mine and swear loyalty to Robin Hood and his companions. Speak up, jolly blade, and never fear – and we'll soon have you as fine a shot with the long bow as you are a player with the stout quarter-staff!'

'Why, here is my hand,' cried the stranger, 'and my heart goes with it, honest Robin. My name is John Little, and you need not fear that I will bring any shame upon you and your merry men: I am skilled in the arts of war and of the chase, and will follow you loyally wheresoever you may lead.'

'I still think you need a ducking!' said Scarlet later that day as they all sat round a fire before which two plump does were roasting. 'But a good sprinkling with brown ale will at least do you no harm. It is our custom here in the green-wood to give every man who joins us a new name. What say you, my friends, shall we not make this into a christening feast for our new friend, and bestow a greenwood name upon him?'

'Well said, good Scarlet!' cried the outlaws, gathering round in a ring of laughing faces. 'And Robin shall be his godfather!'

'Agreed!' smiled Robin. 'Now to your work, good Parson Scarlet!'

'Why then,' cried Scarlet, filling a gigantic mug with foaming ale, 'attend all of you! This child, this babe brought here for christening, was called John Little. But seeing that he is so small, so puny a babe – being indeed no more than seven foot high, and a mere ell or so about the waist (what say you, child, a mere yard and no yard and a quarter? – well, well, a year of venison and strong ale will make you two yards about!) – As I was saying, seeing that the child is so under size –'

'And still under-nourished!' interrupted John Little, sniffing hungrily in the direction of the steaming venison.

'Seeing all this!' continued Scarlet serenely, 'we'll turn him back to front – and name him Little John now and for ever. Long live Little John!'

With that he made as if to pour the ale over his god-child's head, but Little John twisted the mug out of his hand, and shouting aloud: 'Thus Little John pledges Robin Hood and all who follow him in the merry greenwood!' he set the great tankard to his lips and drained it at a draught.

After that, they feasted and rejoiced far into the evening. But thence forward Little John became one of Robin's most faithful followers and truest friends, and in time, as Will Scarlet grew too old for such active service, he became his second in command.

But though he grew no shorter, and certainly no narrower round the waist, the name of Little John stuck to him, nor was he ever known by any other.

How Sir Richard of Legh
Paid the Abbot

ONE day, soon after he came to the greenwood, Little John was wandering with Robin Hood deep in the wilds of Barnsdale. With them were Scarlet and Much, besides a small party of picked bowmen, and they were in search of a hidden site in which to make a camp to which the whole band could retire if Sherwood should prove too dangerous at any time.

When a place was found and the camp was being made, Little John said to Robin:

'Good master, let us shoot a fat deer for our dinner: we should be all the better for a feast!'

'I have no great desire to dine just yet,' said Robin, 'and there is still time to find us a guest for dinner. Do you and Scarlet and Much take bow in hand and go through the woods to the Great North Road which runs not far from here. Wait there in hiding until some uninvited guest passes that way – and bring him to dinner whether he will or no.'

'What kind of guest would you have?' asked Little John who was still unused to Robin's ways.

'Well,' laughed Robin, 'some bold baron, bishop or abbot will pay best for his dinner, or even a proud knight or squire. But look you hinder no honest yeoman nor labouring man, nor set upon any company if there be a woman in it of good and virtuous mien.'

Away went Little John with his two companions and were soon in hiding beside the road. At first there was no sign of any likely man, but at length a knight came riding slowly from the direction of York, his hood hanging over his eyes, and his chin sunk sorrowfully on his chest.

Then Little John stepped out into the road and bowed low before him, catching his horse's bridle in one hand as he did so.

14   'Welcome, gentle knight,' he said. 'To me you

are very welcome. I come with an invitation for you from my master, who waits fasting – as I and my two companions wait also – until you are set at dinner with us.'

'What master is yours?' asked the knight.

'Robin Hood!' answered Little John.

'A noble and a gentle master,' said the knight. 'I have heard tell of him, and right gladly will I be his guest.'

So away they went into the greenwood, and at the camp in Barnsdale, Robin greeted the knight full courteously.

'Welcome, sir knight,' he cried, 'welcome you are indeed. I have fasted three hours in the hope of your company!'

'God save you, good Robin Hood,' murmured the knight, 'and all your merry men too. I will indeed eat my dinner with you – though little appetite have I this day.'

Then, having washed in fair water, and uncovered while Robin said grace, they sat down to a fine meal of venison, with swan and pheasant as 15 side dishes, and many another delicacy with which skilful shooting had provided them.

'I thank you,' said the knight when the meal was ended. 'I have not dined so well these past three weeks. If I come this way again, mayhap I can ask you to dine with me – but there is poor chance of it now.' And the knight sighed sadly.

'Many thanks, kind sir,' answered Robin. 'But now, before you go, I must ask you to pay something towards what you have eaten: the tithe of the forest, we call it. I am but a poor yeoman now, and it has never been good manners to let a yeoman pay for a knight's dinner.'

'Alas,' said his guest, sighing even more deeply, 'my coffers are empty; there is naught that I can proffer without shame.'

'Search his saddle bags, Little John,' commanded Robin. 'You must not blame us, sir,' he added to the knight, 'it is our custom. But tell me truly how much you have.'

'No more than ten shillings,' was the answer.

16   'If you have indeed no more,' said Robin, 'I

will not touch a single penny of it – and if you have need of more, why more will I lend to you.'

'Here,' called out Little John, who had spread a mantle on the ground and emptied the knight's bags on to it, 'here I find but half a pound and no more.'

'The knight is a true man, then,' said Robin. 'Fill him now a cup of good wine, and he may be gone if he will, or stay and tell us his story. For indeed I wonder to see how thin and old his clothes are, and how sad and weary he looks. Sir knight, tell me how this comes about: have you spent all or gambled all away? Did you lose money in usury, or spend it upon women – or has it been stolen from you?'

'By God that made me,' said the knight, 'my wealth was lost by no evil of my doing. My ancestors have been knights this hundred years and more; we held fair lands in Cheshire – four hundred pounds had I to spend in every year, and no name was held in greater honour than that of Sir Richard of Legh. But now I have no goods, save 17 my wife and young children – and they are like to starve.'

'In what manner, noble Sir Richard, have you lost all this?' asked Robin.

'By the cruel craft and usury of the Abbot of St Mary's hard by here,' answered Sir Richard. 'My son set out with King Richard to the Holy Land – and news came but lately that he lay a prisoner, and I must raise a thousand pounds for his ransom, and that right speedily. Six hundred was all that I could come by, till the Abbot lent to me four hundred on the surety of my house and lands: tomorrow is the day that my bond to him falls due. If I do not pay him the four hundred pounds by noon, both house and lands are his. And I have but ten shillings, for I can beg or borrow no more – and what I had raised Prince John's tax gatherers came three weeks ago and took from me. May be they did so at the prompting of the Abbot who, as I know well, longs to take all my lands.'

'What sum do you owe?' asked Robin. 'Tell me as exactly as you can.'

'Just four hundred pounds,' answered Sir Richard.

'And if you do not pay it tomorrow?'

'Why then, I lose my lands, and there is naught for me to do but to go overseas and serve the King in Palestine. It would be a sight to have seen, ere I die, where Our Lord lived and died as a Man, and to have stricken a blow towards freeing His Holy Sepulchre from the unbelieving Saracens; but woe is me for my wife and small children, and for the land which was my father's before me and which I had hoped would be my son's and his heirs' for ever.'

'Have you no friends who can lend you the money?' asked Robin.

'Never a one will own me now, though they were kind enough when I was rich and prosperous,' sighed Sir Richard. 'But now the only surety I can offer for a loan is my word as a 19 knight, and my faith by Our Lady the Holy Mother of Christ.'

'And no better faith could a man have,' exclaimed Robin, crossing himself devoutly.

'Go now to our treasury, Little John, and see if you can there find four hundred pounds. And see also what we can do for clothes such as a knight should wear. And this day twelve-month doubtless he will seek us out in the greenwood and tell us how he fares and what he can give to us in return.'

'Now may God bless you, kind Robin Hood,' said Sir Richard. 'And be sure that this day twelve-month will find me once again in your company.'

The time was drawing towards noon next day, and the Abbot of St Mary's sat in great state in his abbey, with his monks about him, receiving payments of rents from the many tenants who held lands and houses from him.

20   Most of the rents or debts were paid early in

the morning: in a few cases the tenant or the borrower was unable to pay — and then the Abbot rubbed his hands and smiled a fat, contented smile, while his Prior entered a new possession among the Abbey's holdings.

'My lord, there is still the debt of Sir Richard of Legh,' said the Prior when all else had been paid or settled. 'Four hundred pounds did we lend to him, and he vowed to pay it, even to the last penny, by noon today — or else forfeit his fair lands at Legh in Cheshire.'

The Abbot rubbed his hands. 'Many a rich acre!' he chuckled. 'And the fine house of Legh Hall! All ours, all ours!'

'My lord, it wants still half an hour of noon,' the Prior reminded him.

'Tush, tush!' gurgled the Abbot. 'Sir Richard cannot pay! Prince John sent the tax gatherers to him but last month — oh, I have it on sure authority that Sir Richard cannot pay — my good friend Sir Guy of Gisborne saw to that, ha! ha!'

'Yet we must wait until noon,' said the Prior.

'Ah well,' murmured the Abbot, 'but a little while – and then all is ours.' At that moment a monk came swiftly to them.

'Sir Richard is here!' he whispered to the Abbot, 'but in poor array: you need not fear that he can pay his debt!'

Sure enough, Sir Richard came slowly up the hall to where the Abbot sat, and he looked sad enough, and poor enough too in the old and tattered cloak which was wrapped about him. He came before the table at which sat the Abbot with his Prior and his Justice, and knelt down humbly.

'God's blessing, my lord Abbot,' he said. 'I am here upon my hour.'

'Have you brought the money you owe me?' was all that the Abbot could gasp out.

'Not one penny,' sighed Sir Richard, and hung his head.

'Indeed, you are a sorry debtor!' cried the 22 Abbot with a great sigh of relief, and then turning to the Justice, he exclaimed: 'Drink to me, my friend! Wish me luck, good sirs!

'But what do you here?' he added, turning quickly back to Sir Richard. 'If you have not brought my money back, why have you come at all?'

'To beg for longer grace,' answered Sir Richard humbly. 'Bethink you, my lord Abbot – my son is prisoner to the wicked Saracens: he was taken fighting at good King Richard's side, and for the benefit of Holy Church. Surely Holy Church will grant me but six months more to clear the debt – which I can do in that time.'

'No, no,' broke in the Justice. 'Your time is up. You must pay or forfeit!'

'Now, good Father Prior,' begged Sir Richard, 'stand you my friend and beg grace of the Abbot!'

'Nay, not I!' cried the Prior.

'Then, my lord Abbot,' pleaded Sir Richard, 'at least hold my land in trust until I have found 23 the money, and I will be your true servant and serve you faithfully.'

'No, by God!' shouted the Abbot. 'You get no further help from me, false, perjured knight that would cheat Holy Church of four hundred pounds. Get you gone out of my Abbey, ere I bid my serving men whip you from the door like a stray cur!'

'You lie, Abbot!' cried Sir Richard, drawing himself up suddenly. 'I am no false knight! But for you, a servant of God, to suffer a knight to kneel before you and beg your charity – you are shamed for ever!'

'Get hence!' shouted the Abbot, purple with rage. 'Your lands and houses are mine! Hark – the clock strikes twelve!'

'The clock strikes twelve,' said Sir Richard quietly, 'and I have paid my debt!'

As he spoke, he flung back his cloak, showing that he was well and richly clad beneath it. Then he laid four leather bags on the table in front of 24 the Abbot, and stood silent.

The Abbot's jaw dropped and the colour fled from his face.

'Count the money,' he said in a shaking voice. The Prior did so, and found it exact.

'Now,' said Sir Richard, 'the land is mine again, and all the cruel Abbots in England cannot prove otherwise!'

With that he strode from the Abbey, while the Abbot stood and cursed him, threatening vengeance when the time should come.

But Sir Richard rode full speed to Legh Hall where his wife was waiting anxiously for him.

'Be merry, good lady!' he cried. 'All is saved – I am free from the Abbot. We have but to dwell quietly at home for a year, and I can save enough to pay back kind Robin Hood who lent me the money.'

'And I will pray for Robin Hood,' said the Lady of Legh.

Maid Marian of Sherwood Forest

GAMWELL HALL, seat of Robin Hood's uncle Sir William Gamwell, was not far from Nottingham, and thither Sir Guy of Gisborne rode one day attended only by his squire.

Sir William welcomed Sir Guy, and after feasting him well, suggested that he should come with him next day to the great Gamwell festival held not far away in the forest.

Hoping to find out where Robin Hood was, Sir Guy agreed readily to this. But of course he said no word of his real reasons either to Sir William or to young Will Gamwell who rode with him.

It was a merry scene in the green glade of the forest: young men and girls dancing round the Maypole, barrels of ale broached for Sir William's tenants, and many a game or contest for young and old alike.

26   Sir Guy sat quietly under a tree with old Sir

William watching it all, and only once did he lean forward suddenly with an angry glint in his eyes, and that was when young Will Gamwell led out one of the maidens to dance whom he recognized suddenly as the Lady Marian Fitzwalter disguised as a peasant girl.

'What maiden is she who dances with your son?' asked Sir Guy.

'That?' answered Sir William vaguely. 'Oh, she is known as the shepherdess Clorinda: she is often at these feasts, but really I can tell you little of her!'

'You mean you won't tell me!' thought Sir Guy as his host hastily changed the conversation. 'I am certainly on the right trail now!'

Later in the day came a band of foresters in Lincoln green and there was a great contest of archery in which 'Clorinda' took part as well and seemed as good an archer as any of them.

Sir Guy mounted his horse and rode casually down to the butts to watch the sport. As he drew near, Clorinda discharged her arrow, and a cheer 27 went up from all who were watching since she had shot it into the very centre of the gold, which was the middle ring of the target.

'I must needs shoot well indeed to equal that, fair Clorinda,' said the chief of the foresters stepping forward and setting an arrow to his string. The arrow sped, and another cheer arose, for everyone could see that it too had struck within the ring of gold, so close to that of Clorinda that the points were in contact and the feathers were intermingled.

'I claim your hand, fair Queen of the May,' said the forester bowing low before Clorinda, and with a blush and a smile she held out her hand to him and he led her away into the dance.

But Sir Guy had recognized the forester, and now he turned to Will Gamwell who stood beside him.

'What is that archer's name?' he asked.

'Robin, I believe,' said young Gamwell carelessly. 'I think they call him Robin!'

'Is that all you know of him?'

'What more is there to know?'

'Why, let me tell you,' said Sir Guy sternly, 'that he is none other than the outlawed Robert Fitzooth, called Earl of Huntingdon; and there is a large reward offered to any man who can bring him prisoner before the Sheriff of Nottingham.'

'Is he really?' said Will Gamwell, as if not in the least interested.

'He would be a prize well worth taking.'

'I expect so.'

'Shall we not take him then?'

'You may if you please.'

'But are your tenants and followers not loyal?'

'Loyal they are indeed!'

'Then,' exclaimed Sir Guy, growing more and more angry, 'if I were to call upon them in the King's name, would they not aid and assist?'

'Assuredly they would,' answered Gamwell, 'on one side or the other!'

'But I have Prince John's warrant for the arrest of Fitzooth,' said Sir Guy. 'What would you then advise me to do?'

'Why,' answered Gamwell calmly, 'I would advise you to turn round and ride your hardest for Nottingham – unless you want a volley of arrows, a shower of stones and a hailstorm of cudgel-blows to help you on your way!'

On hearing this, Sir Guy's squire clapped spurs to his horse and went away at full gallop – which gave Sir Guy an excuse for galloping away after him shouting:

'Stop, you rascal!' until they were out of sight of the Gamwell gathering.

They did not draw rein then, however, but made all speed to Nottingham where Sir Guy roused the Sheriff with the news that Robin Hood was within a few miles with scarcely a dozen men.

Within half an hour he was off again, accompanied by the Sheriff and an armed band, hurrying along the road towards Gamwell.

The sun was sinking as they came to a bridge across the river and on the further side saw a
30 small party of foresters and men at arms headed

by the shepherdess Clorinda who still carried her bow, and by whose side now walked the gigantic form of Brother Michael Tuck, lately of Fountains Abbey.

'Now who be these that come riding so fast this way?' bellowed the Friar. 'False traitors all, I'll be bound – yes, there I perceive Sir Guy of Gisborne to whom the sacred dues of hospitality are unknown, and with him the Sheriff of Nottingham – loyal servant of whoever pays him the fattest fees!'

'Out of the way, renegade Friar!' shouted Sir Guy angrily, for the Friar and his party had reached the bridge first. 'And you, Lady Marian, hasten away to Arlingford, for you are in truly doubtful and traitorous company.'

'You mistake, false knight, you mistake!' declared the Friar calmly. 'The lady here is the fair Clorinda, well known throughout the forest of Sherwood as the Queen of the Shepherdesses. As for the doubtful and traitorous company – I see none of it on *this* side of the bridge!'

31

'Out of the way!' echoed the Sheriff angrily. 'We seek Robert Fitzooth, known as Robin Hood, who but an hour since was consorting with you not far from this spot!'

'By the Rood, you'll not pass this way,' bellowed the Friar, 'until you have made full apology to the fair Clorinda and myself for all terms, taunts, and other words of slander uttered in the hearing of these good fellows!'

'Force them aside!' cried Sir Guy impatiently. 'Robin Hood is escaping us even now! And catch that froward girl for me: Lord Fitzwalter will reward me well when I bring her back to him!'

Sir Guy raised his hand derisively as he spoke, and swift as thought Clorinda raised her bow, the string hummed, and Sir Guy's hand was transfixed by an arrow.

'Treachery! Cut them down!' shouted the Sheriff. The bow-string hummed again, the Sheriff's horse reared up as an arrow whizzed 32 into the ground between its forefeet, and the

Sheriff fell backwards out of the saddle and sat heavily down in a large pool of mud.

Thereupon arrows sped amongst the Sheriff's men, who rushed up the steep bridge, only to be beaten back by the mighty staff in the hands of the great Friar. For, roaring lustily, he stood there alone, whirling his staff from side to side among the Sheriff's men, knocking down one, breaking the ribs of another, dislocating the shoulder of a third, flattening the nose of a fourth, cracking the skull of a fifth, and pitching a sixth into the river, until the few who were lucky enough to escape with whole bones clapped spurs to their horses and fled for their lives – the outraged Sheriff leading the way, and the wounded Sir Guy of Gisborne bringing up the rear, amidst the laughter of the fair 'Clorinda' and her followers and the jeers and taunts of the Friar.

Next morning Lord Fitzwalter was disturbed over his breakfast by the loud blast of a trumpet and the sounds of a general alarm. Hastening to the castle gate, he saw a large body of armed men drawn up on the further side of the moat, with a herald blowing a trumpet and an officer bidding them 'Lower the drawbridge, in the King's name!'

'What for, in the devil's name?' roared Lord Fitzwalter angrily.

'Be it known to all just men!' proclaimed the herald, 'that the Sheriff of Nottingham lies in bed grievously bruised, many of his men are like to die of divers injuries and the good knight Sir Guy of Gisborne is sorely wounded by an arrow. And we charge Sir William Gamwell, the Lady Marian Fitzwalter and one Friar Michael lately of Fountains Abbey, as agents and accomplices in the said riot, and traitors for that they have aided and consorted with the outlaw Robin Hood, otherwise Robert Fitzooth sometime of Locksley Hall.'

'Agents and accomplices!' spluttered Lord Fitzwalter. 'What do you mean by coming here 34 with this nonsensical story of my daughter the

Lady Marian bruising the Sheriff, injuring his men and shooting arrows into Sir Guy of Gisborne! Off you go, or I'll bid my men shoot at you with their crossbows!'

'You will hear more of this!' shouted the officer in command of the troop. 'Not so lightly may you flout the will of our liege lord Prince John!'

'Then let him come in person,' shouted Lord Fitzwalter, 'or send someone whom I can trust. How know I that you are not some of these very Sherwood outlaws in disguise, trying to gain entrance to my castle under cover of the King's name and a silly story about my girl bruising sheriffs and shooting men-at-arms!'

The troop of men, seeing that an archer with a crossbow stood ready at every loop-hole, that the drawbridge was up, and the moat both wide and deep, retreated with many threats in the direction of Nottingham.

Lord Fitzwalter at once summoned his daughter, and on demanding the truth, Marian 35 confessed that she was known in the Forest as the shepherdess Clorinda, and told the story of Sir Guy's defeat at Gamwell bridge.

'You go no more forth from the castle!' declared Lord Fitzwalter.

'Then I get out if I can,' answered Marian firmly, 'and am under no obligation to return.'

'Away with you to the topmost turret chamber!' ordered her father. 'No one will get you out of there!'

'Prince John will do so,' said Marian, with a shudder. 'I hear that he is now at Nottingham – those were his men before the castle even now. He saw me on the eve of my wedding to Robin of Locksley, and it is said that he has sworn to take me – and perhaps not hand me over to Sir Guy as readily as he has promised.'

'I'll defy a wicked Prince as surely as a wicked knight,' shouted Lord Fitzwalter.

'You cannot withstand Prince John,' said Marian. 'Think of the power he can command. He'll sack the castle, hang you from the nearest

tree – and take me whether you will or no . . .
But if you shut me up – and I escape from the
castle, no blame can be attached to you, and you
can welcome him here with every sign of regret,
for my absence and fury at my flight.'

'Hum! Ha!' Lord Fitzwalter opened his mouth
to swear, but shut it again as he realized the truth
of what Marian said.

'Then if you – er – escape,' he asked, 'do you
go to Sherwood Forest as half wife of this outlaw
Robin Hood?'

'I go to Robin Hood,' answered Marian
quietly, 'but until King Richard returns from
Palestine, pardons him and restores him to his
rightful position, I dwell in Sherwood Forest as
Maid Marian – promised but not united to
Robin. And this he has sworn by God and
Our Lady, and here and now I re-affirm the
oath.'

Lord Fitzwalter thought for a few minutes.

'Robin or Robert, he's a true and honourable
man,' he said at last. 'And you are my daughter, 37

and would bring no dishonour upon our line . . .
God bless you, Marian . . . Go to your room
now – and do not let anyone see you leaving
Arlingford Castle, or it will be the worse for us
all!'

When, a few hours later, Prince John rode up
at the head of a hundred men, Lord Fitzwalter
met him at the gate with the most profuse expres-
sions of loyalty, begged pardon for his behaviour
to the herald in the morning, and placed the
whole castle at his disposal.

'I am honoured, deeply honoured, your Royal
Highness,' he said, still on his knees. 'There is no
guest more welcome than yourself – and your
trusty followers. Had you but sent sure proof
with your herald this morning, I had admitted
him at once: but with this cursed outlaw Robin
Hood so nearby, one must be careful. Why, he
came in disguise into Nottingham itself and rescued one of his ruffians from the very foot of the
gallows!'

Prince John was graciously pleased to accept

Lord Fitzwalter's apologies, and his hospitality at the same time. But when he asked to be presented to the Lady Marian, it was found that she was no longer in her room.

Then Lord Fitzwalter raged round the castle, cursing the carelessness of his followers and threatening dreadful things to the guards who had let her pass. But nothing could be learned of her whereabouts, though one guard volunteered the information that a young archer had been seen standing in the gatehouse an hour or so before Prince John's arrival – and that youth was missing also.

Prince John graciously lent half his followers to Lord Fitzwalter, and they scoured the neighbourhood for several days. But the Lady Marian Fitzwalter had vanished.

Hearing that Prince John was at Nottingham with a whole troop of his followers, Robin Hood walked near the edge of Sherwood disguised as a Forest Ranger. He hoped to meet some traveller coming from Nottingham, fall into conversation with him, and learn of Prince John's movements or intentions.

Presently, as he strolled along the road, he met a young man dressed in forest attire who held a bow in his hand, carried a good quiver of arrows on his back and wore a stout broadsword at his side.

'How now, good fellow!' cried Robin in a harsh voice. 'Whither away so fast? What news is there today in the good city of Nottingham?'

'I go about my own business,' replied the young man, 'and the news is that Prince John has come to Nottingham to put down the outlaws in the forest.'

'About time, too,' said Robin, remembering that he was posing as a Ranger, or keeper of the Royal Deer. 'And what do you, my fine lad, with that long bow and those goodly arrows?'

'I mind my own business,' answered the youth, 'which I would that other wanderers in Sherwood did likewise!'

'My business is with such as you,' said Robin sternly. 'Tell me your name and business, or my sword must enforce it.'

'Two can play at that game,' cried the youth, and flinging down his bow and quiver, he drew his sword and stood on the defence. Robin did likewise, and a minute later the blades clashed together.

Very soon Robin found that his antagonist was at least his match in all the skill and practice of swordsmanship, though weaker in the wrist than he, and not so heavy in the sheer weight of blows.

They fought for some time without either gaining much vantage, though the blood was running down Robin's face, and his antagonist was wounded in the arm.

'Hold your hand, good fellow – let us fight no more,' said Robin at last, stepping back and leaning on his sword, quite forgetful of his pretended role as Forest Ranger. 'You fight too well to be wasted like this: come, throw in your lot with Robin Hood and be one of his merry men.'

'Are you Robin Hood?' gasped the youth.

'Robin Hood I am, and no other!' was the reply.

'Oh, Robin, Robin! Do you not know me?' cried his late antagonist with a sudden change of voice.

'Marian!' gasped Robin. 'And I wounded you, and knew you not!' In another moment his arms were around her.

'Welcome to Sherwood,' he said at length, when she had poured out all her tale to him. 'Come away with me now to our secret glen, and let Scarlet and Much, Little John, and the rest, welcome their queen – as I do; and swear, as I do, to be true and faithful servants now and henceforward to you, Maid Marian of Sherwood Forest.'

There was feasting and rejoicing that night in
the secret glade where Robin and his merry

men did honour to their lovely queen. There was no lack of good roasted venison, great flagons of wine were set on the board, bowls of brown ale, and many another delicacy.

When the feast was ended, Robin rose with a great flagon in his hand.

'My friends!' he cried. 'Let us drink first, now as ever, to King Richard – King Richard and his speedy return from the Crusade!'

When the pledge was drunk, Robin rose again.

'And now!' he cried, 'drink to our Maiden Queen! To the Lady Marian! Let us pledge ourselves once more to the true service of God and His Holy Mother, as true Christian men should. But let us also even as true knights to their lady, pledge ourselves that all our actions shall be so pure and so far from all evil that we do nothing we should think shame of were it done in the presence of our queen, our Maid Marian!'

'Maid Marian of Sherwood Forest!' cried 43

every man there, springing to their feet. 'To our King and Queen of the Forest – to Robin Hood and Maid Marian!'

The Coming of Friar Tuck

SUMMER had come and gone, and the leaves were turning brown in Sherwood, when on a day as Little John and Scarlet and the pick of Robin's men practised archery and quarter-staff in the secret glade, Marian said suddenly:

'Robin, it grieves and surprises me that we have heard nothing of good Brother Michael.'

Robin nodded thoughtfully. 'He surely knows that you dwell now in the forest,' he said, 'for he did you good service on the day of the Gamwell feast when Guy of Gisborne and the Sheriff tried to take me.'

'That was indeed a strange encounter,' Marian remarked. 'He came suddenly along the river bank waving his mighty staff – and disappeared as suddenly after the fray, without speaking a word to me.'

'Your father forbade him to visit you at Arlingford?' queried Robin.

Marian nodded. 'And the Abbot of Fountains Abbey cast him out also,' she added. 'He said he would live a hermit in some cell by the river, as plain Friar Tuck.'

Robin thought for a little while, and then with an exclamation he called Will Scarlet to him:

'Scarlet, what was it you were saying not many days since of a hermit living in the cell at Copmanhurst?'

'He's a mighty man,' said Scarlet, 'who looks far too well fed – and well drunk also – to be a hermit. But he dwells there all alone by the river, and for a penance he carries any traveller across the river at the ford there – though I doubt not but that he asks a good fee for his ferrying. It is said also that he will fight, on a challenge, with the quarter-staff, and crack the crown of any man who dares stand against him.'

'Now!' cried Robin, 'I swear by the Virgin that I will go tomorrow and seek out this hermit. If he prove to be Michael Tuck, so much the better, and if not we will at least have a round at crown-cracking. If he be a good fellow, and a virtuous priest as well, we would be the gainers by his presence amongst us here in the forest.'

Next morning accordingly Robin disguised himself as a wandering minstrel, though without forsaking either bow or sword, and set out through the forest in the direction of Gamwell.

He turned aside when he came to the river and followed it for some time until he came to the ford of Copmanhurst. And there sure enough was a boat moored to the further side, while a wisp of smoke rising among the rocks showed that the hermitage built against the cliff edge was inhabited.

'Ho-la! good ferryman! Ho, there!' shouted Robin.

'Who calls?' answered a deep voice, and a gigantic friar strode out upon the river bank. He was dressed in a brown robe such as all friars wore, but it was well girdled about with a curtal 47 of cord at which hung a huge broadsword. On his head, in place of a hood, the friar wore a round steel head-piece, while the sleeves rolled back showed great muscular arms far better suited to a warrior than a priest.

'Now then, my fine fellow!' shouted Robin, 'come and ferry me over the river!'

'All in good time, my son, all in good time!' boomed the friar, and seizing a mighty staff he stepped into the boat and poled it across to where Robin stood.

'A mere minstrel!' he grumbled as Robin stepped aboard. 'He could have swum it – and the wetting would have done him good. Alas for my vow!'

When they reached the other side the friar sprang quickly on shore and turned to his passenger.

'Now then,' he cried, 'let me see how your purse is lined!'

'Surely, good hermit,' said Robin mildly, 'you 48 would not turn robber?'

'Not so,' answered the friar, 'I do but ask for alms – as is the Church's due!'

'No man is compelled to give alms,' Robin reminded him, 'save only by his conscience.'

'A good doctrine,' agreed the friar, 'but the office of a priest is to awake the conscience – which I will now proceed to do with my good staff across your shoulders – unless your conscience should be awake already!'

'Come then and search my purse,' said Robin, pretending to cringe in fear. The friar dropped his staff and advanced unsuspectingly, and Robin suddenly whipped out his sword and held it to the friar's throat.

'For that, base hermit,' he cried, 'you shall carry me across the river once more – and this time it shall be upon your back! And no fee shall you receive for so doing, save a cracked sconce, if you again demand any.'

'A bargain,' said the friar calmly, 'for the water is low, the labour is light – and the fee such a one as I relish!'

49

The friar bent down and Robin, still with the drawn sword in his hand, mounted on his back. Walking as if he took no note of his burden, the friar strode down into the water and made his way across by the ford until he had brought Robin safe and dry to the other bank.

Here, however, he pitched him to the ground so suddenly that he was forced to drop his sword to save himself from falling.

'Now then, my fine fellow,' said the friar, setting his foot on Robin's blade and drawing his own as he spoke, 'you must carry me back across the river – and I'll crack your sconce in payment when we get to the other side.'

'Turn and turn about!' cried Robin cheerfully, and he bent his back and took up the enormous weight of the friar. It was hard labour indeed, even for so strong a man as Robin, for the friar must have weighed nearly twenty stone; but he carried him down to the river and waded slowly and carefully into the middle of the stream.

'A good mount, truly!' crowed the fat friar,

chuckling to himself at Robin's exertions. 'This puts me in mind of a fable writ by the learned Aesop of the two simpletons who carried their ass home from the market town!'

'Yes,' panted Robin. 'But it reminds me more of another fable – that of the ass with the bags of salt. That was a better example, and a wiser – or so it seems to me.'

And as he said this, Robin gave a sudden dextrous jerk and flung the friar over his head into the deepest part of the river. Then he sprang hastily to the bank and turned back to laugh heartily at the great fat figure floundering and blowing like a whale in the water his bald scalp covered in green slime and chickweed.

'Fine fellow, fine fellow!' spluttered the friar scrambling to shore at length. 'Make ready now and I will pay you the cracked sconce I owe you!'

'No, no!' laughed Robin. 'I have not earned it. But you have earned it, and you alone shall have it.'

After that they set at one another with great staves, smiting and feinting and raining blows like two lusty farmers threshing the corn.

At last they paused through sheer weariness — and though neither was beaten, both had paid the toll of a broken sconce.

'Honour, me thinks, is satisfied!' puffed the friar. 'Let us shake hands and part friends. You are a stout fellow for a minstrel, by the rood!'

'I have used sword as well as harp,' answered Robin. 'But never have I met with such a wielder of the cudgel as you are. So a truce to our quarrel, and come let us rest a while in your cell — where, doubtless, you can set food and drink before a poor wanderer.'

'Alas,' said the friar, looking suddenly meek and pious. 'There is no food here fit for a man such as yourself. You are welcome to share the frugal diet of a poor hermit vowed to fasting and prayer.'

With that he led Robin to the hermitage, 52 which was no more than a rough hut of stone and wood with a thatched roof, built across the front of a cave in the low cliff which fringed the river at that point.

Inside were but a table, a couple of stools, a crucifix hanging on the wall, and a bed of leaves and dried grass at the back of the shallow cave. The friar reached down a dish of pease from a shelf of rock, set it on the table, and poured water out of a jug into a couple of drinking horns.

'It seems, holy brother,' said Robin, seating himself on a stool and sampling a mouthful of the pease without much enjoyment – 'It seems that a few pease and a jug of water have thriven you marvellously. Surely it is a miracle when a man who lives upon a handful of pease is yet round and red-faced – and as lusty a fighter as you have shown yourself to be!'

'Ah, good minstrel,' answered the friar with a deep sigh, 'it has pleased Our Lady and my patron saint, the holy Dunstan, to bless exceedingly the pittance to which I restrain myself.'

'Aye, but there is no such blessing granted to poor wayfarers like myself,' said Robin. 'Surely some kindly forest ranger visits you from time to time and leaves some store for the use of travellers – which they are doubtless as ready as I am to pay for in other coin than the ferry fee!'

So saying he flung a piece of gold on the table, and eyed the friar with a merry twinkle in his eye. The friar looked at the coin hungrily, hummed and hawed for a while, and then going to the side of the cave opened a cupboard cunningly concealed in the rock and drew out an enormous venison pasty. He set it on the board, and Robin set to work to satisfy his hunger at such a speed that the pasty began visibly to shrink.

The friar sat watching him, his face growing longer and longer as the pasty grew shorter and shorter, until at last Robin took pity on him and exclaimed:

'Good friar, far be it from me to tempt you
into breaking your vows of abstinence, but surely

good manners demand that a host should partake of the same dish as his guest – if only to show that the dish is wholesome and harmless!'

'By the rood!' cried the friar, his eyes lighting up. 'Long sojourn alone in a hermit cell had make me forget that excellent rule! A thousand apologies, my worthy guest.'

With that he set to work on the other end of the pasty – cramming in two mouthfuls for every one that Robin could take – and before long the dish was empty.

'Holy man,' said Robin gravely, 'I'll wager another piece of gold that the same forester who left that pasty here for the good cheer of travellers, left also a stoop of wine for their further refreshment! I think that if you were to search your cupboard again, you would find that I was right.'

The friar rose to his feet with a broad grin – which he tried in vain to transform into a look of pious reproach – and set before his guest a leathern bottle containing at least a gallon. From this he filled the two horns, and then said:

'Sir stranger, pledge me in this, and, as in duty bound, tell me your name.'

'Right willingly,' answered Robin, 'but once again you forget that you are my host, and a man must know the name of his bounteous entertainer.'

'I am but the plain Hermit of Copmanhurst,' was the answer, 'and my name is Friar Tuck!'

'Then, good Friar Tuck!' cried Robin. 'Good Brother Michael that was, I drink to you – I Robin Hood, who once also had another name. Waes hael, Friar Tuck!'

'Drink hael, Robin Hood!' answered Friar Tuck, draining his horn at a single draught. 'Right glad am I that the minstrel should hide so good a man.'

'Come back to Sherwood with me, jolly Friar,' begged Robin. 'I have come hither to seek you, with a summons from the Lady Marian, whose confessor you were. Truly, when you broke my head with your staff I guessed you were the man I sought – but when you made such short work of the venison pasty, I knew that I was right!'

'With all my heart!' bellowed Friar Tuck, pouring out another horn full of wine. 'Farewell to pease and spring-water! You live well in the forest, jolly Robin, or so it is said. That you need a priest there is no shadow of doubt: and that I am the priest you need, no one will dare to deny!'

Robin meanwhile had stepped to the door of the hermitage and sounded the call to his men.

'Drink another draught before we go!' shouted Friar Tuck. 'It would be a sad pity to leave behind so good a wine. Here's to you, Robin Hood; and here's to our life in merry Sherwood!'

And with that he drained another horn, and sang right lustily:

Oh, bold Robin Hood is a forester good,
As ever drew bow in the merry greenwood:
At his bugle's shrill singing the echoes are ringing,
The wild deer are springing for many a rood:
Its summons we follow, through brake, over hollow,
The thrice-blown shrill summons of bold Robin Hood!

Penguin Children's 60s

ALI BABA AND THE FORTY THIEVES • *Retold by N. J. Dawood*
THE AMAZING PIPPI LONGSTOCKING • *Astrid Lindgren*
ANNE AT GREEN GABLES • *L. M. Montgomery*
AT THE RIVER-GATES AND
OTHER SUPERNATURAL STORIES • *Philippa Pearce*
CLASSIC GHOST STORIES
CLASSIC NONSENSE VERSE
THE CLOCKWORK MOUSE • *Dick King-Smith*
DEAD MAN'S LANE • *Joan Aiken*
THE DRAGON ON THE ROOF • *Terry Jones*
FOUR GREAT GREEK MYTHS • *Roger Lancelyn Green*
THE GREAT MOUSE PLOT AND
OTHER TALES OF CHILDHOOD • *Roald Dahl*
THE GREAT TIME WARP ADVENTURE • *Jon Scieszka*
THE HOOLIGAN'S SHAMPOO • *Philip Ridley*
KEEP IT IN THE FAMILY • *Anne Fine*
KING ARTHUR'S COURT • *Roger Lancelyn Green*
THE LITTLE MERMAID AND
OTHER FAIRY TALES • *Hans Andersen (Translated by Naomi Lewis)*
LOST DOG AND OTHER STORIES • *Penelope Lively*
THE MIDNIGHT STORY • *Margaret Mahy*
MOOMINTROLLS AND FRIENDS • *Tove Jansson*
MRS PEPPERPOT TURNS DETECTIVE • *Alf Prøysen*
THE NIGHT TRAIN: STORIES IN PROSE AND VERSE • *Allan Ahlberg*
THE PIED PIPER OF HAMELIN AND OTHER CLASSIC STORIES IN VERSE
ROBIN HOOD AND HIS MERRY MEN • *Roger Lancelyn Green*
SHERLOCK HOLMES AND THE SPECKLED BAND • *Sir Arthur Conan Doyle*
SMACKING MY LIPS • *Michael Rosen*
TALES FROM ALICE IN WONDERLAND • *Lewis Carroll*
TALES FROM THE JUNGLE BOOK • *Rudyard Kipling*
THREE QUIRKY TAILS • *Paul Jennings*
TOM SAWYER'S PIRATE ADVENTURE • *Mark Twain*
TOM THUMB AND OTHER FAIRY TALES • *Jacob and Wilhelm Grimm*